# ZAYDE COMES TO LIVE

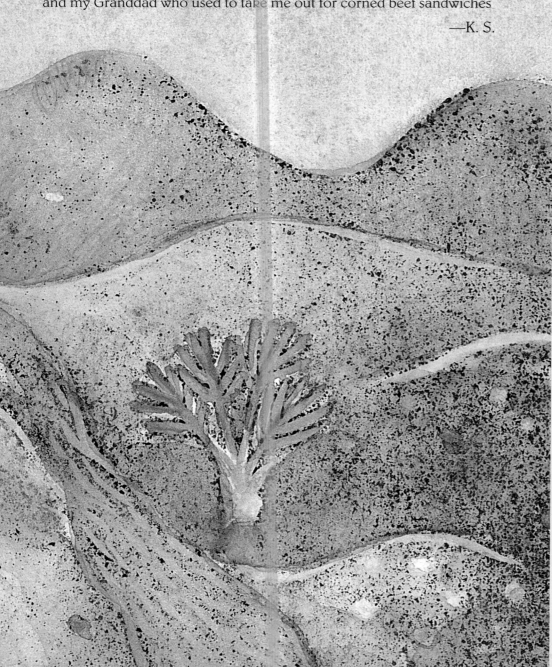

For all my beloved grandchildren—sons of my sons:

Aaron and Debbie's Brayden Raine and Logan Casey,

Rudi and Esther's Akiva Gilad and Hillel David,

and Joshua and Julia's Elon Max

—S. S.

In memory of my Grandpa who taught me how to row a boat,

and my Granddad who used to take me out for corned beef sandwiches

—K. S.

Published by
PEACHTREE PUBLISHERS
1700 Chattahoochee Avenue
Atlanta, Georgia 30318-2112

www.peachtree-online.com

Text © 2012 by Sheri Sinykin
Illustrations © 2012 by Kristina Swarner

Illustrations are linoleum prints with watercolor and colored pencil. Title typeset in Adobe's Belwe Medium by George Belwe for Schelter & Giesecke; text typeset in FontShop International's AdvertRough-Two by Just van Rossum.

Book design by Maureen Withee and Loraine M. Joyner

Printed and manufactured in May 2012 by Imago in Singapore
10 9 8 7 6 5 4 3 2 1
First Edition

Library of Congress Cataloging-in-Publication Data

Sinykin, Sheri Cooper.
  Zayde comes to live / written by Sheri C. Sinykin ; illustrated by Kristina Swarner.
    p. cm.
  Summary: When Rachel's beloved grandfather, Zayde, comes to spend his last days with her family, she worries what will happen when he dies, especially after friends tell her the Christian and Muslim beliefs about the afterlife.
  ISBN 13: 978-1-56145-631-4 /  ISBN 10: 1-56145-631-4
  [1. Future life--Fiction. 2. Death--Fiction. 3. Grandfathers--Fiction. 4. Jews--United States--Fiction.] I. Swarner, Kristina, ill. II. Title.
  PZ7.S6194Zay 2012
  [Fic]--dc23
                                            2011020977

# ZAYDE COMES TO LIVE

WRITTEN BY **SHERI SINYKIN**            ILLUSTRATED BY **KRISTINA SWARNER**

PEACHTREE
ATLANTA

**Z**ayde comes to live with us. It's because he is dying.

No one says this, but I know from what they do not say. From what Zayde cannot do anymore, like play hide and seek around the house. Or ball in the yard.

Now he lives in a
sleeper-chair in our
living room. The sun
wakes him each
morning.

He watches squirrels in the trees.

And movies on TV.

And me.

When we play catch, he gets tired and Mama says, "Don't throw balls in the house, Rachel."

When we read, he gets out of breath and I say, "It's okay, Zayde. Let me."

Megan says Zayde will go to Heaven, a happy city in the
clouds with pearly gates and diamond streets and more
light than we can imagine. First, Zayde must believe in
Jesus, but we do not.

Hakim says Zayde will go to Paradise, where milk-and-honey rivers flow in gardens of pomegranates and dates. First, he must believe in Allah, but we do not.

That's because we are Jewish.

I worry for Zayde. Where will he go?

I am afraid to ask.

Sometimes I watch him sleep to make sure
he wakes up again. His nurse comes to check on
him. And Rabbi Lev comes to check on us all.

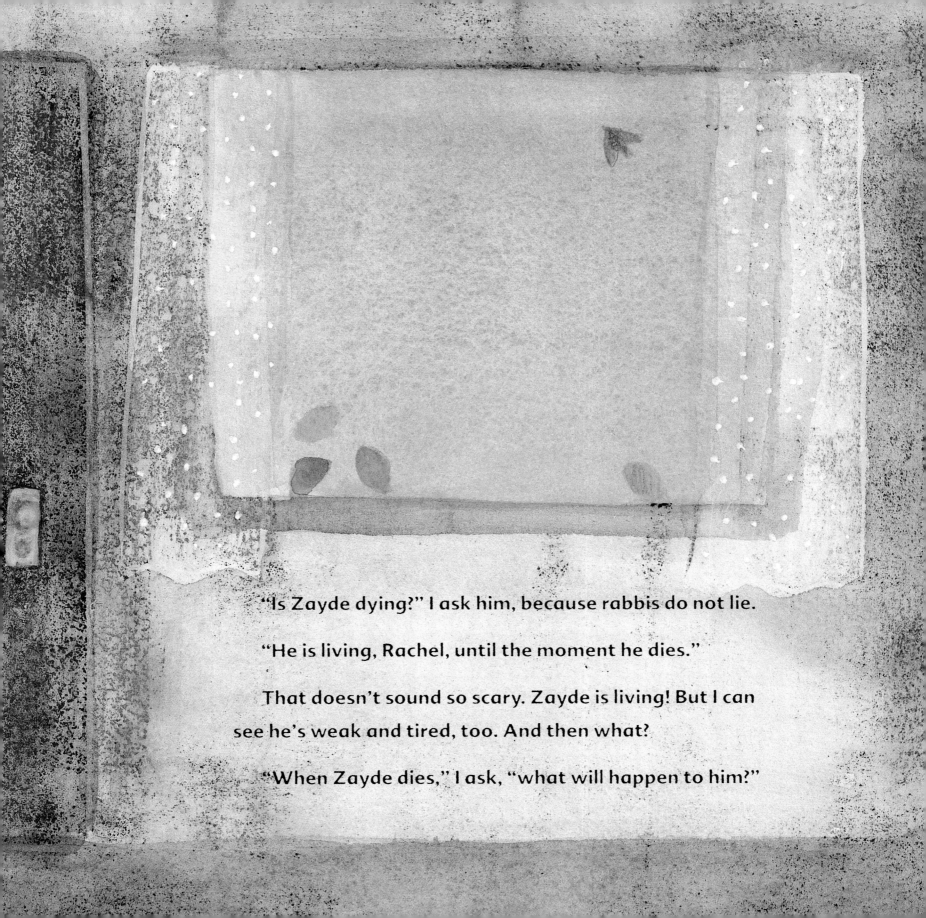

"Is Zayde dying?" I ask him, because rabbis do not lie.

"He is living, Rachel, until the moment he dies."

That doesn't sound so scary. Zayde is living! But I can
see he's weak and tired, too. And then what?

"When Zayde dies," I ask, "what will happen to him?"

"He'll take one last breath," Rabbi Lev says. "Then his energy will live on with your ancestors in the World to Come— what we call *Olam Ha-Ba.*"

I close my eyes and try to make a picture. I see a zooming, happy Zayde with his mama and daddy, his bubbe and his own zayde, and all the aunts and uncles I never knew.

After Rabbi Lev leaves,
I touch Zayde's hand. When he
looks up at me, I see doll's
eyes, not his regular sparkly
blue ones.

"It's me, Zayde. Rachel."

He blinks and blinks.
Finally, he laughs. "Looks like
you went and grew up while
I was dreaming." Then he pats
the chair, and I snuggle into the
free space beside him.

"What were you dreaming about, Zayde?" I ask.

"The day you were born. What a blessing your first breath was! How happy we were!"

I watch his chest go up and down. I think about first breaths and last breaths, one happy, one sad.

"I don't want you to die, Zayde." My voice whispers like his air-machine.

His arm tightens around me. "It's the circle of life, sweet girl."

I see a new light on his face. "Then you're not scared?"

"I am at peace," he says. "You know the word *shalom?*"

"What we say for 'hello' and 'good-bye'?"

"Yes. But it really means 'peace and completeness.'"

"I don't ever want to say good-bye, Zayde."

"You don't have to, *Rachela*," he says.

"But where will you go?" I ask at last.

"My body is getting tired. I know you can see this. Soon that outside part of me will return to the earth."

I remember how we buried my cat Curry in the backyard. How we hugged and cried and told stories about him.

Maybe we will do that for Zayde, too.

I'll tell about the birdhouse we made,
how he let me paint it purple.

Mama will tell about Zayde's first snow angel, when she was little.

And Daddy will tell how Zayde saved their wedding day with a needle and thread. So many stories.

"But what about the inside part of you?" I ask. "What happens to that?"

Zayde sucks a long noisy breath. "My spirit will live on. This I believe. Because my love will stay here with you, and so will your memories. Always."

I walk my fingers over the blanket until they find his. Then I bury my face against him. Sweet Zayde smells— peppermint and lime.

I know we are making another memory for me.

Breathing in, breathing out,
together, as long as we can.

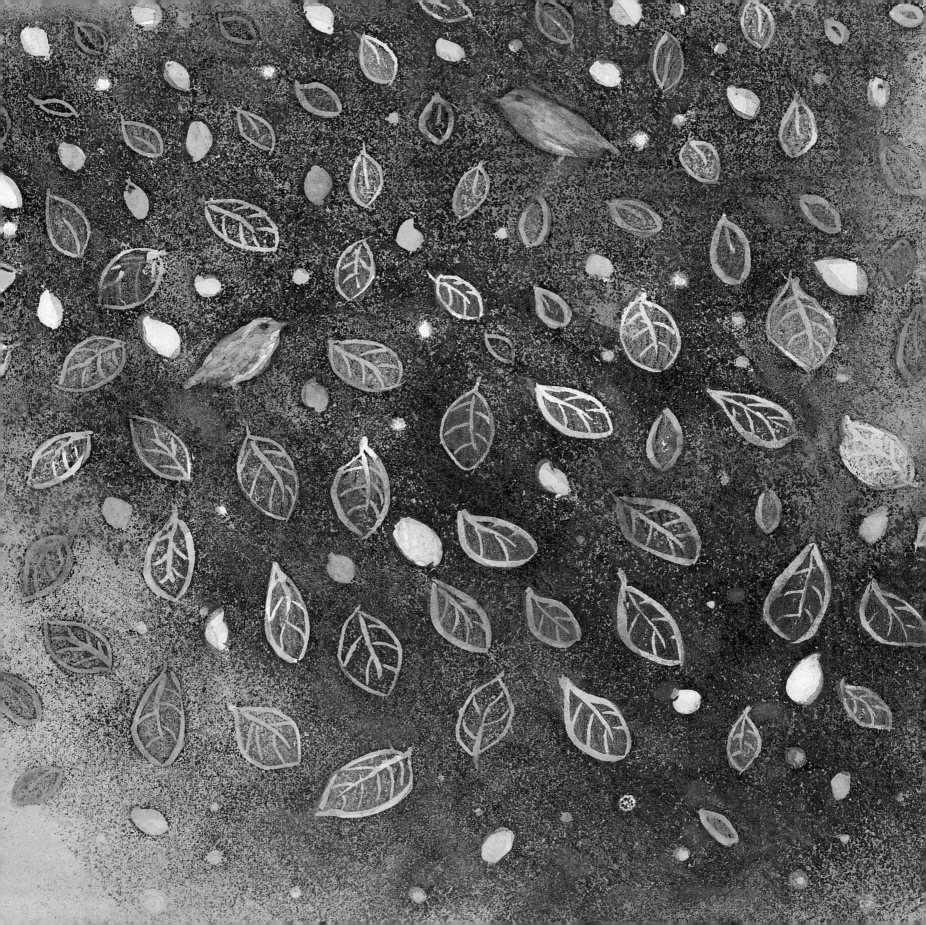

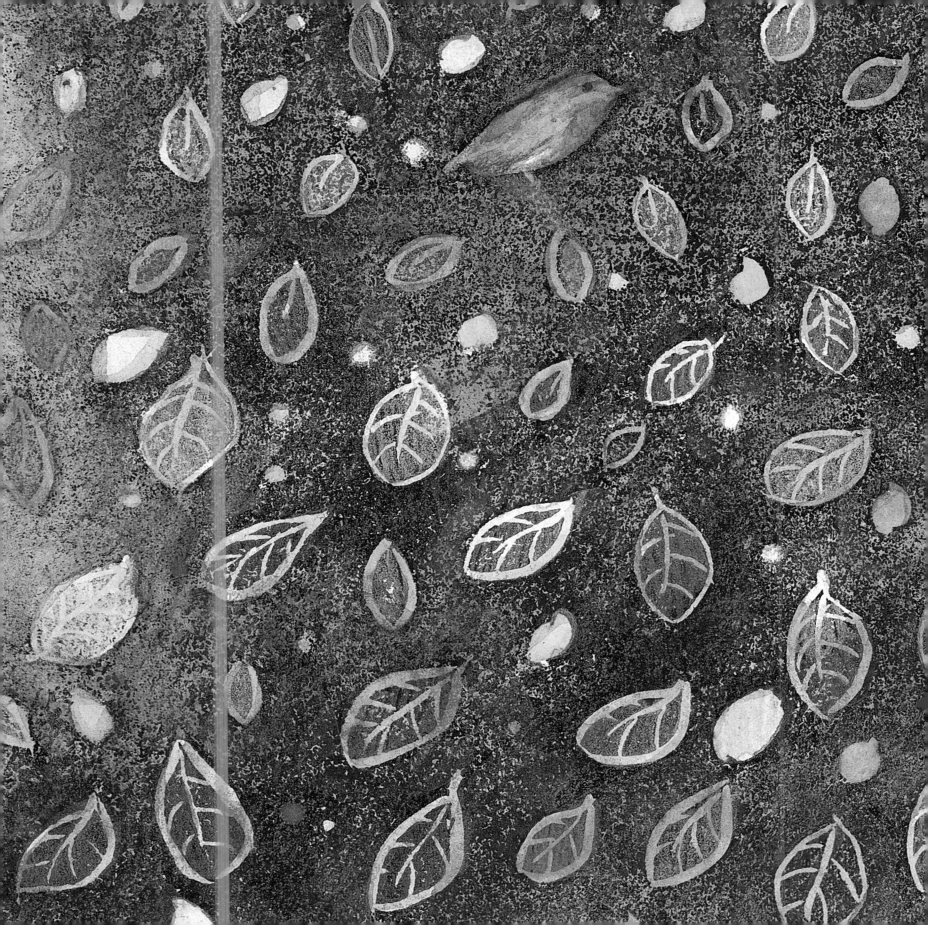